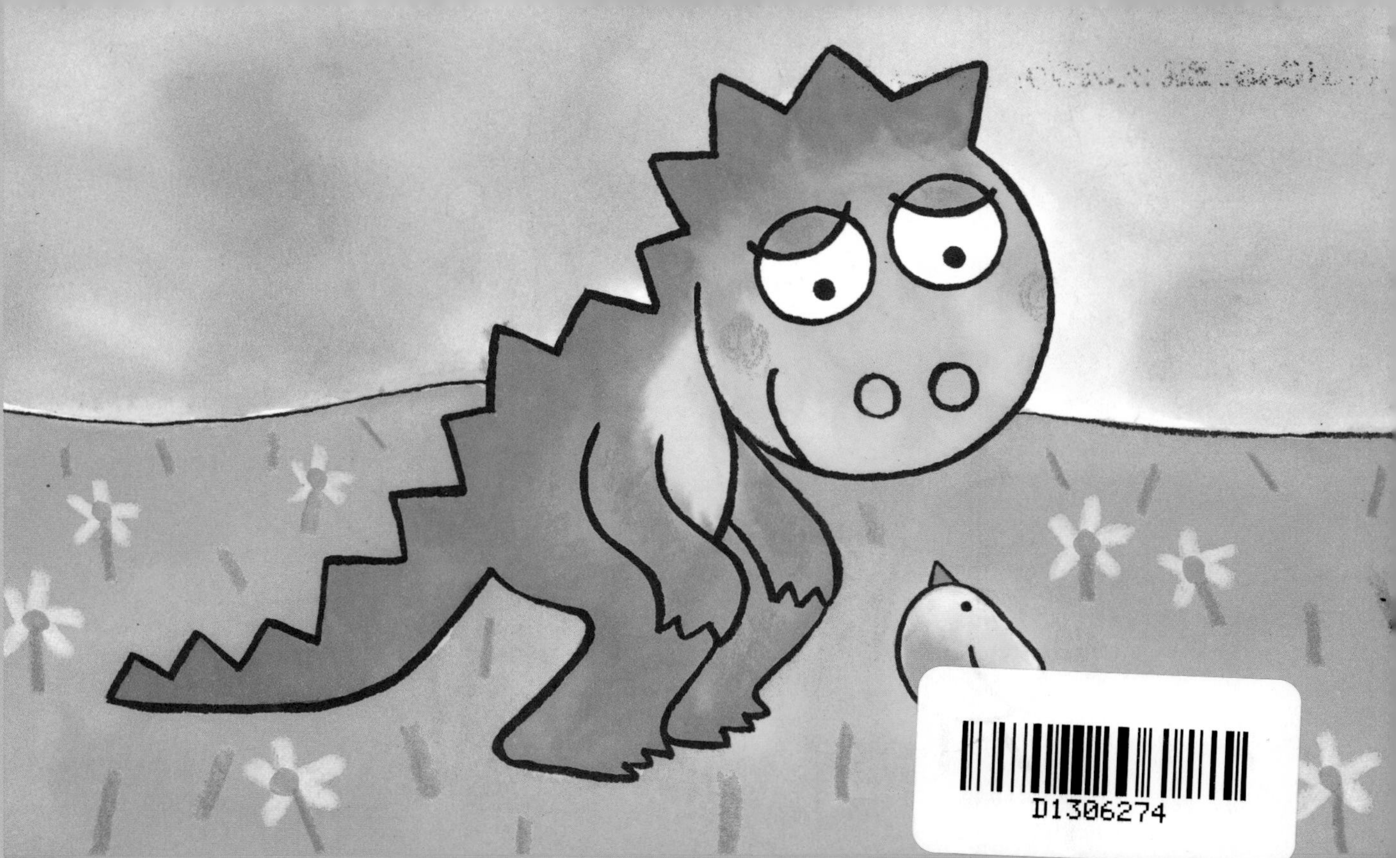

Dinah Dinosaur sees a little bird.

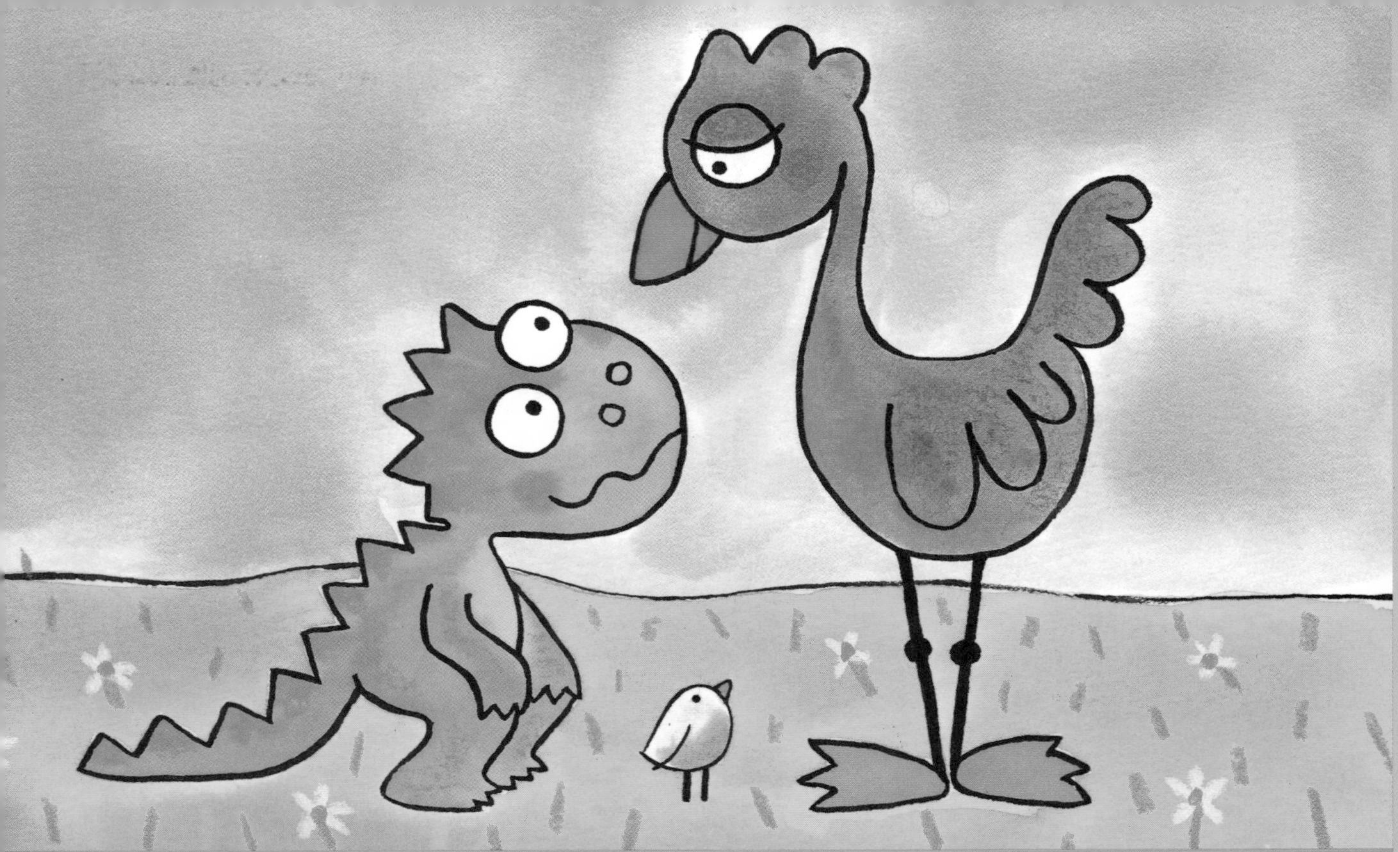

She sees a big bird.

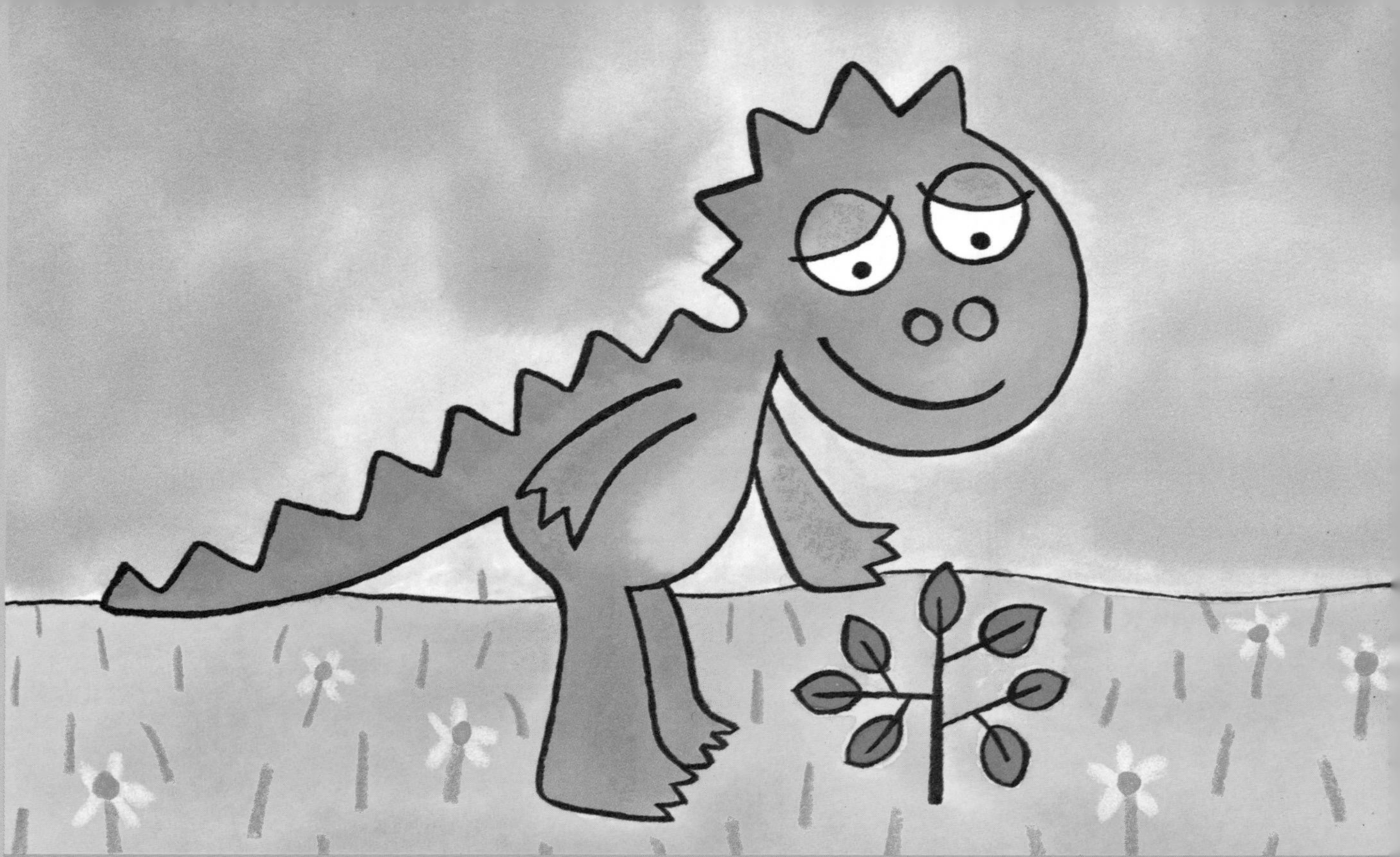

She sees a little tree.

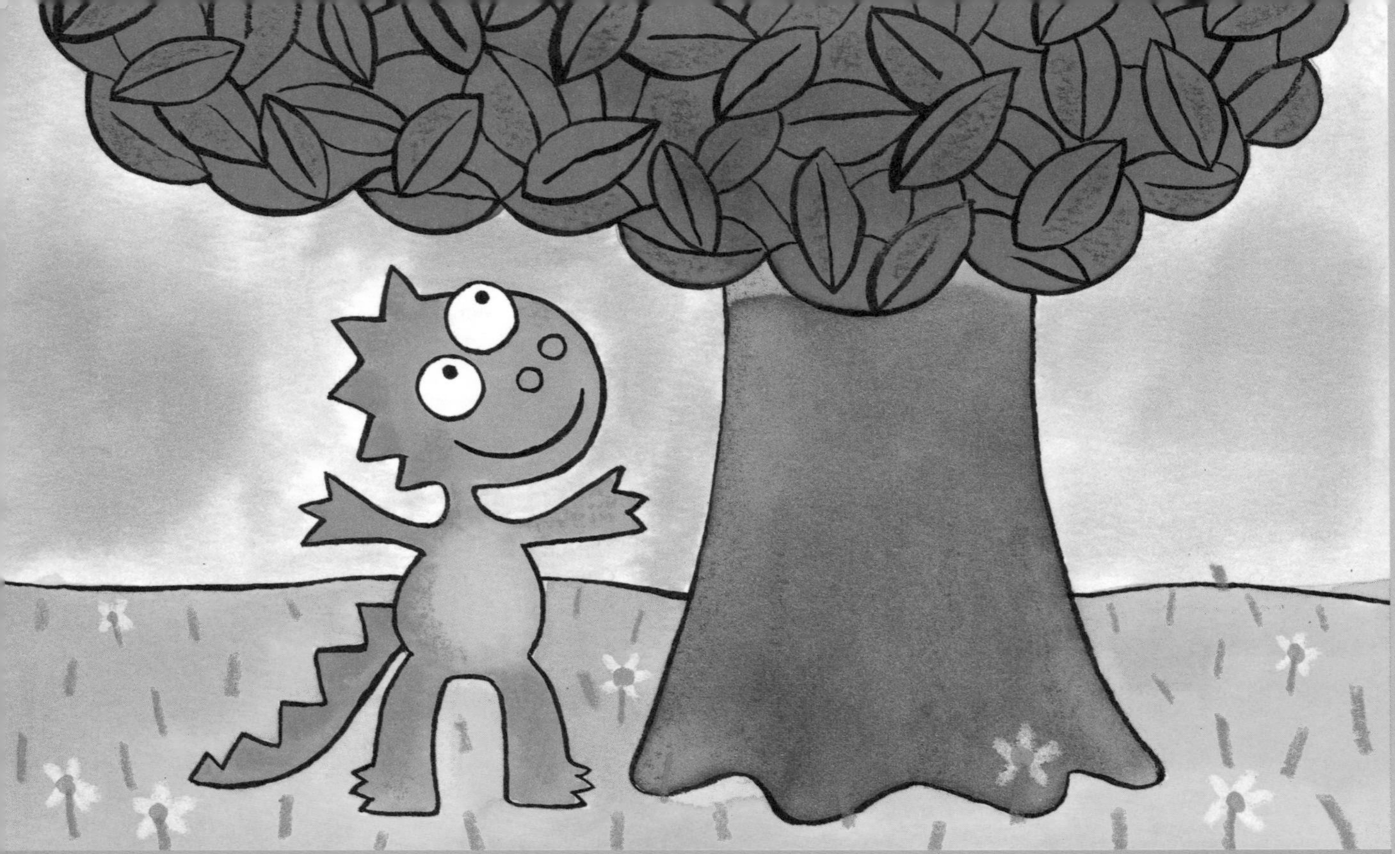

She sees a big tree.

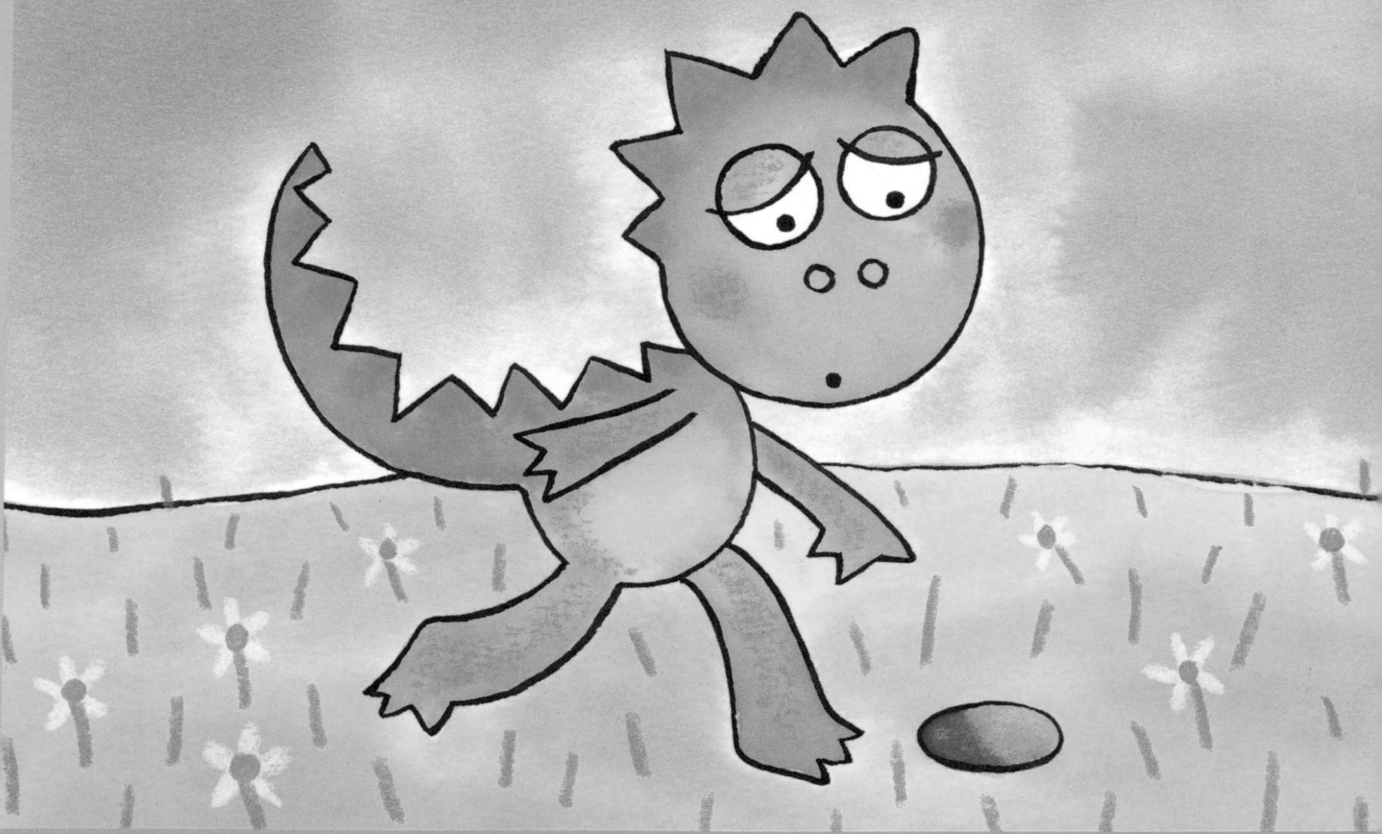

She sees a little hole.

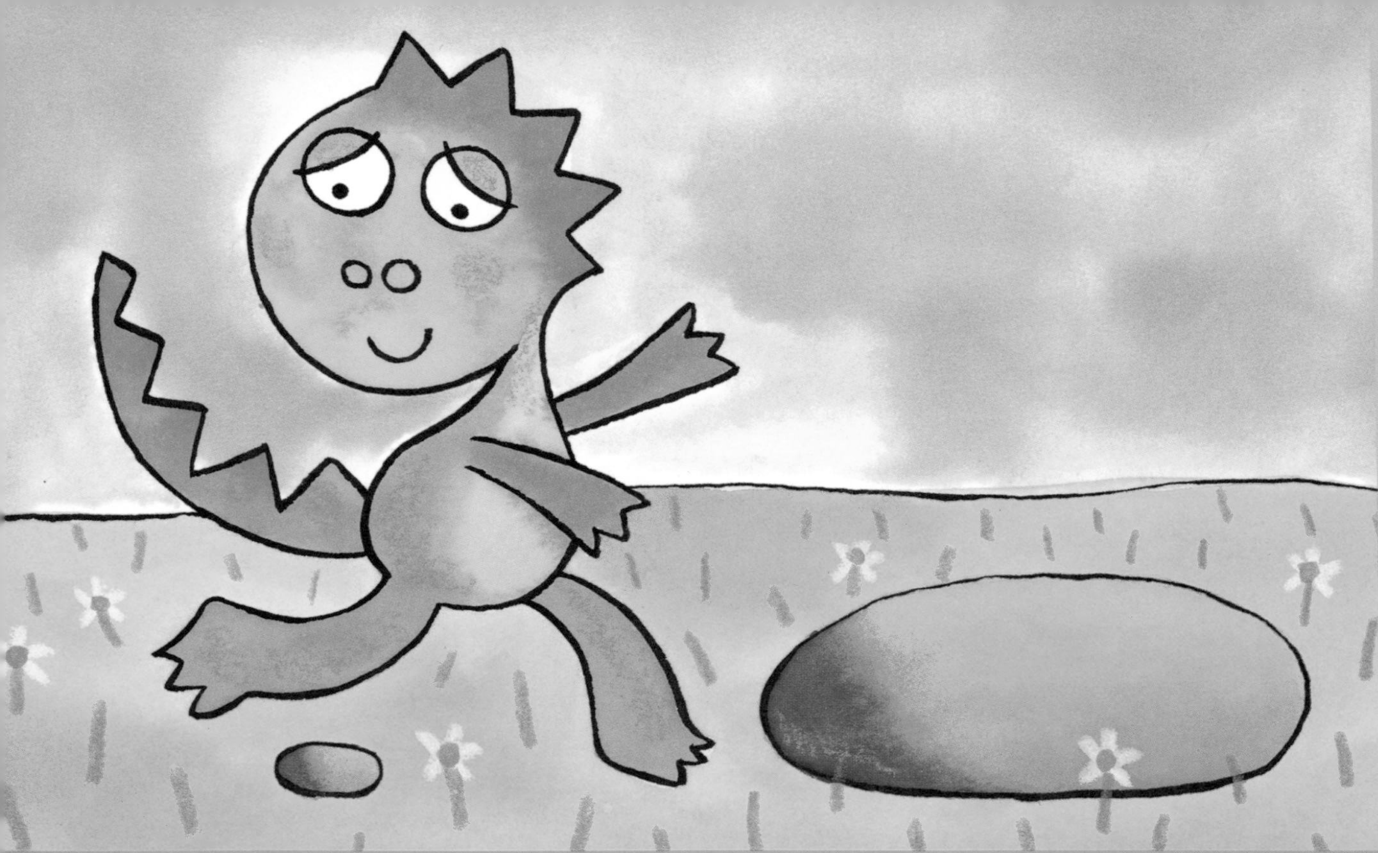

She does NOT see the big hole.

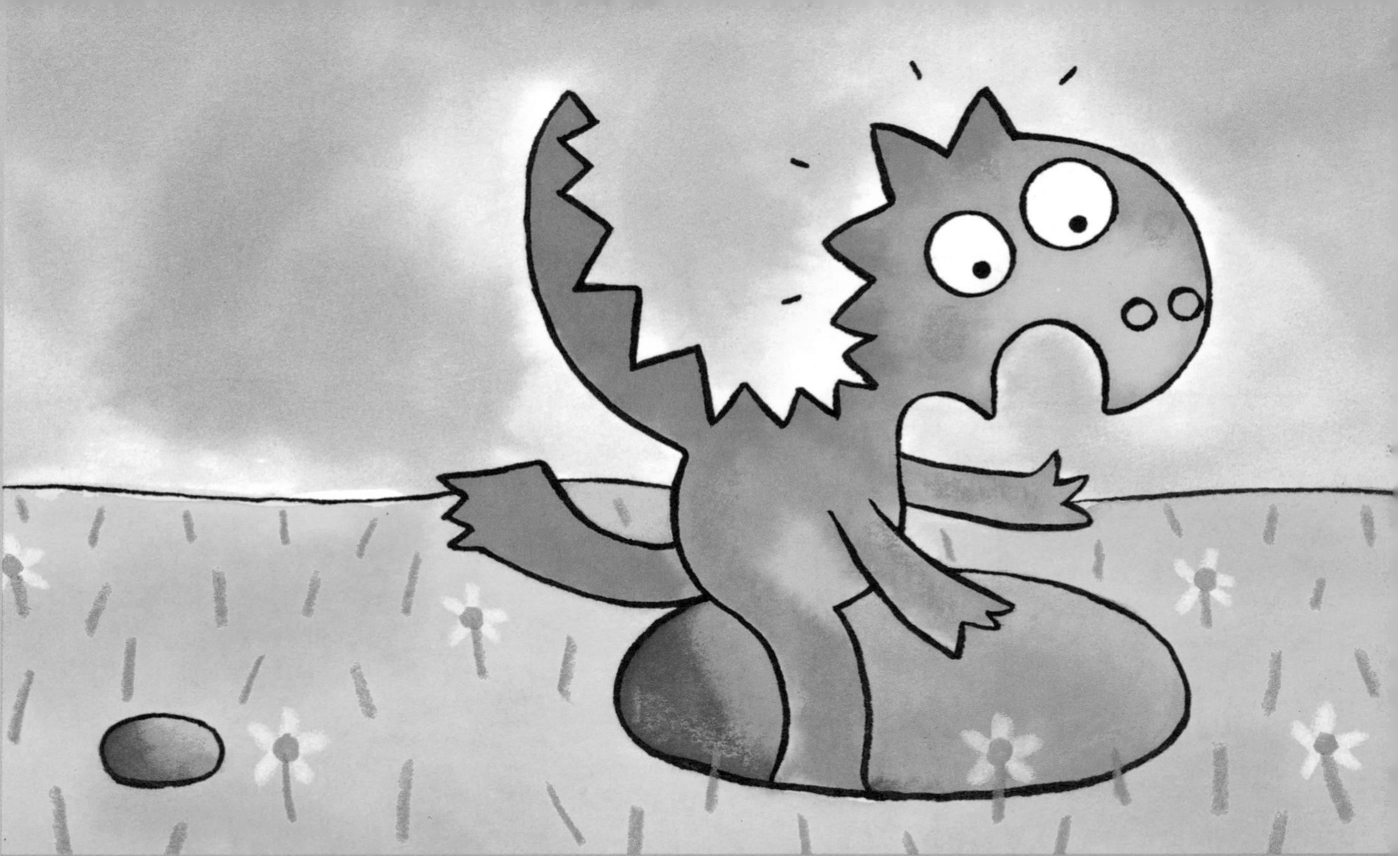

She falls in.

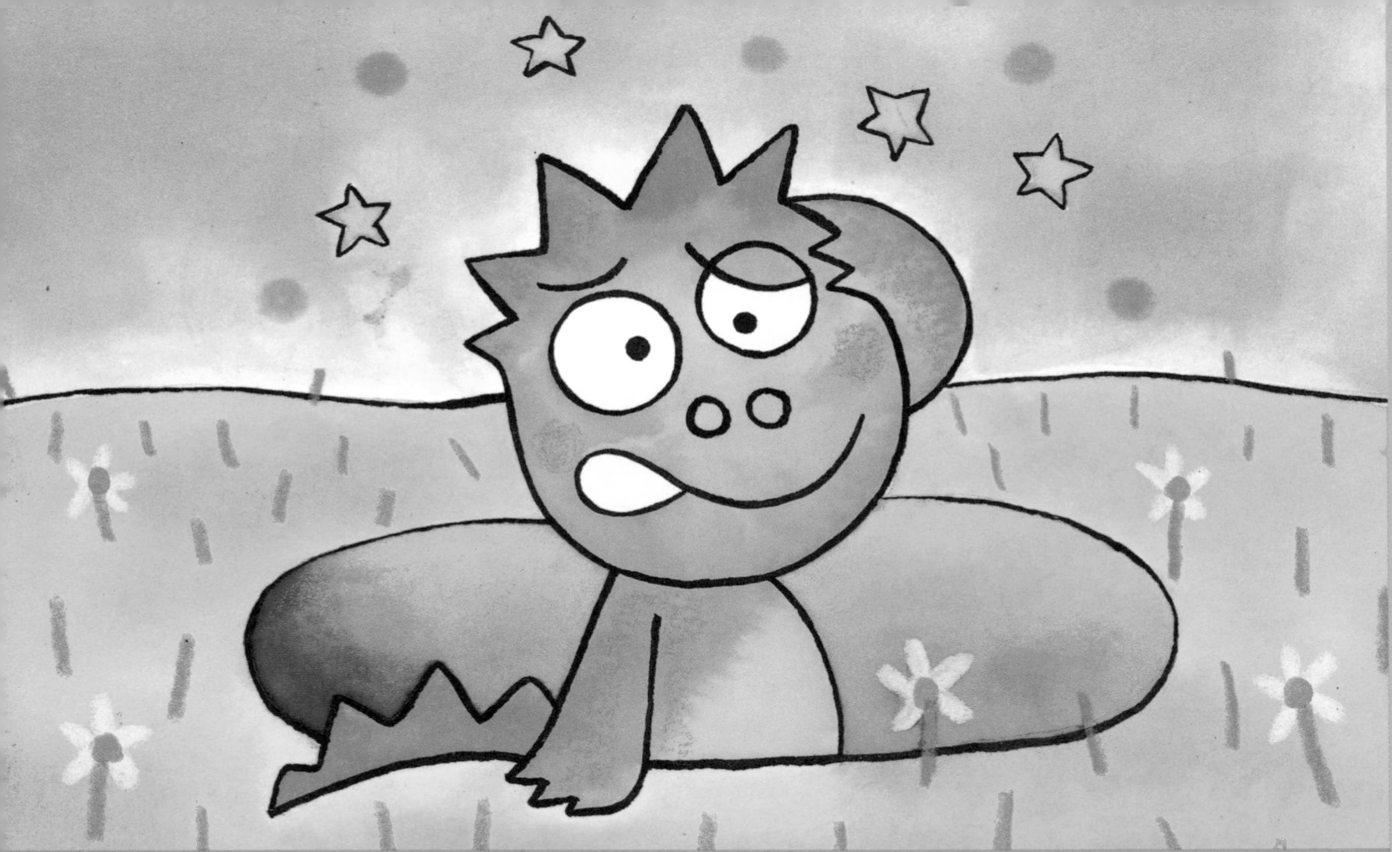

OUCH!